3

3

D0518615

Grafton Books
A Division of the Collins Publishing Group
8 Grafton Street, London W1X 3LA

Published by Grafton Books 1986

A TEMPLAR BOOK
Devised and produced by Templar Publishing
Old King's Head Court, Dorking, Surrey RH4 1AR

Savage, Deborah
    Bird's Nest.— (The Adventures of Peregrine Piecrust; v.2)
    I. Title II. Forsey, Chris III. Series
    823'.914 [J] PZ7

ISBN 0-246-13001-6

Origination by Positive Colour Ltd, Maldon, Essex
Printed and bound in Great Britain by Purnell and Sons
(Book Production) Ltd, Paulton, Bristol. Member of BPCC plc

PEREGRINE PIECRUST IN

BIRD'S NEST

Written by Deborah Savage
Illustrated by Chris Forsey

GRAFTON BOOKS
A Division of the Collins Publishing Group

LONDON GLASGOW
TORONTO SYDNEY AUCKLAND

Peregrine Piecrust hated having his hair cut.

Every month his mother would take him to the hairdressers where his hair would be combed and cut and washed and brushed.

One day, Peregrine decided that he had had enough. Instead of sitting quietly while the hairdresser snipped away, he leapt out of the chair and raced off down the road.

"Come back this minute," yelled his mother as she chased after him. But Peregrine wouldn't listen.

He just carried on running towards home with his wet, soapy hair leaving a trail of bubbles behind him.

"I'm not having my hair cut ever again!" he shouted.

Peregrine Piecrust had made up his mind.

When Peregrine got home, he went straight upstairs to his bedroom and locked the door. He didn't even appear when it was time for tea.

"Just leave him alone," said Mr Piecrust. "He'll learn to do as he's told sooner or later."

So they all carried on eating without him.

As the weeks wore on, Peregrine's hair became longer and longer.

It became so long that he had to have an extra chair to rest it on while he did his lessons.

It became so long that he had to have a trailer fitted to his bicycle so he could tow his hair behind him.

And it became so long and heavy that his neck started to ache if he stood up for too long.

One morning, Peregrine was just getting out of bed when he heard a sort of tweeting noise.

What on earth could it be?

Then he heard it again. "Tweet! Tweet! Tweet!" it went.

Peregrine looked under the bed and on top of the wardrobe. There was nothing there. "Tweet! Tweet! Flutter! Flutter!" went the noise.

He was just looking behind his dressing table when...

SOMETHING DREADFUL HAPPENED!

Peregrine suddenly caught sight of himself in the mirror.

There, perched on the top of his head was the most gigantic black crow!

"Help! Help! Help!" shrieked Peregrine. "There's a great big bird on my head!"

Peregrine's parents came running up the stairs.

"Oh no!" gasped Mrs Piecrust when she set eyes on her son. "There's a nest in your hair."

"Well get it off, quick!" shouted Peregrine who was most alarmed.

Mr Piecrust clambered on to a chair to investigate.

"It can't be done, I'm afraid," he said. "There are six eggs up here and they can't be disturbed until they've hatched."

And he and Mrs Piecrust went downstairs to finish their breakfast.

Peregrine couldn't believe it. What was he going to do?

Luckily, it was Saturday so Peregrine did not have to go to school. Instead, he went to the shops with his mother.

Everybody stared as they walked round the supermarket and very soon there was a huge crowd following them. Peregrine felt very silly indeed.

A photographer even came from the local newspaper to take an exclusive picture.

"Watch the birdie," said the photographer.
And everybody laughed ...
except Peregrine.

The days went by and soon the eggs hatched into six fluffy chicks. They loved living on Peregrine's head but he had some terrible headaches from the noise they made.

Gradually, the chicks grew wings and learned to fly. They still nested in Peregrine's hair though, and liked to slide down his nose on to the dinner table or perch on his ears and flap their little wings.

Then one morning the chicks decided it was time for them to leave. They were going to live in the local park with lots of other crows.

Peregrine was rather sad to see them go, even though they promised to come back and visit him. He waved them off, one by one, until they were just black specks in the distance.

And then can you guess what he did?

He marched straight down to the hairdressers and had his hair combed and cut and washed and brushed. And he never let his hair grow long and tangly ever again.

In fact, he had the neatest hair in all the school.

Well, for a while anyway...